MARiSABiNA RUSSO

Waiting for Hannah

Greenwillow Books New York

GOUACHE PAINTS WERE USED FOR THE FULL-COLOR ART.
THE TEXT TYPE IS KABEL BOOK.

PRINTED IN HONG KONG BY SOUTH CHINA PRINTING CO.
FIRST EDITION   10 9 8 7 6 5 4 3 2

LIBRARY OF CONGRESS CATALOGING-IN-PUBLICATION DATA
RUSSO, MARISABINA.
WAITING FOR HANNAH / BY MARISABINA RUSSO.
P.   CM.
SUMMARY: HANNAH'S MOTHER DESCRIBES HOW
SHE SPENT THE SUMMER SHE WAS WAITING FOR HANNAH TO BE BORN.
ISBN 0-688-08015-4.
ISBN 0-688-08016-2 (LIB. BDG.)
[1. BABIES—FICTION.
2. MOTHERS AND DAUGHTERS—FICTION.]
I. TITLE. PZ7.R9192 Wai 1989
[E]—DC19
87-37201   CIP   AC

WITH LOVE FOR MY DAUGHTER,
HANNAH CARINA STARK

One day Hannah and her mother were on
a very long line at the grocery store.

The lady ahead of them had a huge, round belly.
She was going to have a baby.

"Mama, did you look like that when you were going to have me?" asked Hannah.
"Oh, yes!" said her mother. "I was so big and it was such a hot summer."

"What did you do while you waited?" asked Hannah.
"At the beginning of the summer Grandma gave me
an envelope of morning glory seeds to plant on
the windowsill. She couldn't remember if the
flowers would be blue or pink.

Every day I opened the window and watered the box. That window didn't get too much sun, so I had to wait a long time before the seeds even sprouted.

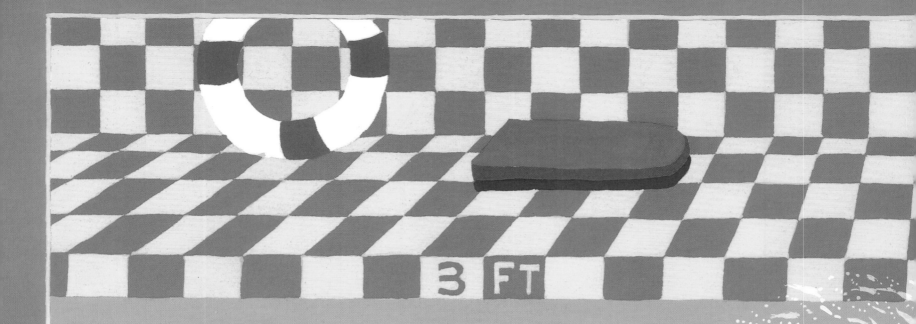

It was such a hot summer. I would take the bus downtown
so I could go swimming at the YMCA. I wore a special
bathing suit and swam laps back and forth, thinking
about you all the while.

In the evenings Daddy and I would take
walks in the park with our dog.
Daddy would throw sticks for her while
I sat on a swing.

A few times we went to the shore and
spent the day at the beach.
We always ended up having a big dinner
of clams or lobster before we went home.

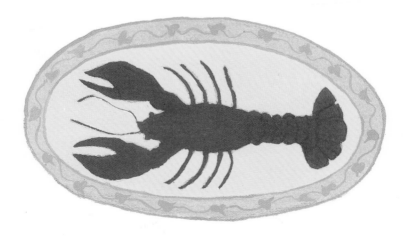

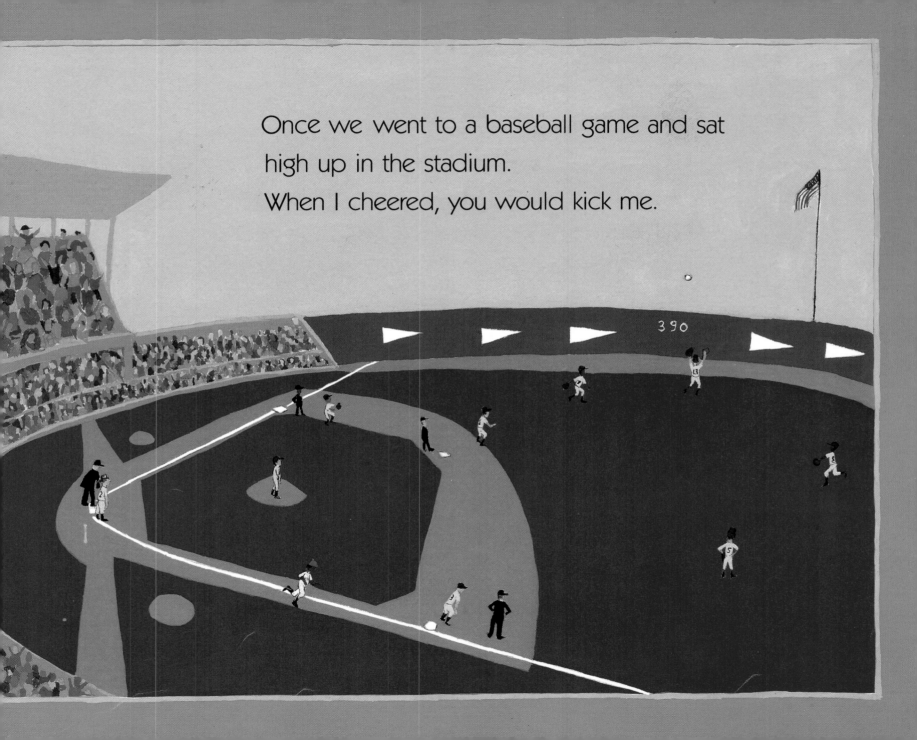

Once we went to a baseball game and sat
high up in the stadium.
When I cheered, you would kick me.

The morning glory vines were growing tall and
gangly, and they wrapped themselves around
the sticks I had put in the box.
Toward the end of the summer they finally
got some buds.

One Sunday Grandma gave a party for me in her backyard. We ate hamburgers and hot dogs and watermelon.

Everyone brought a gift for you: a little chair, a yellow sweater, a bowl for cereal, a tiny fork and a tiny spoon.

Daddy and I watched the morning glories.

They had fat buds, but not one flower as yet!

We couldn't wait for you to be born.

And then on a cloudy Wednesday morning
I felt you coming and we went to the hospital.
You were born, round and perfect, and with
lots of brown hair."

"What about the morning glories?" asked Hannah.

"Oh, the morning glories! When I got home
from the hospital one bud had blossomed.
It was a beautiful pink flower."